Picture Book of Classical Chinese Tales

中国传统故事美绘本（中英文双语版）

Nezha Conquers the Dragon King

从前有一位镇守陈塘关的大将军名叫李靖。他的妻子怀胎三年六个月，生下一个圆圆的肉蛋。家里人谁也没见过这么奇怪的事情，议论纷纷。

李靖认为这是不祥之物，便拔出剑来劈了过去。哪知那肉蛋竟从中间裂开，金光四射，跳出个神气活现的小男孩。李靖一见不禁又惊又喜。

There was once a senior general by the name of Li Jing garrisoned at Chentangguan Pass in the northwest of present-day Sichuan Province. Having been pregnant for as long as three years and six months, his wife finally delivered something resembling a flesh ball. The new life was so peculiar in appearance and so strange that it sent Li's family members into a frenzy of speculation.

Believing it to be an ill omen, Li Jing drew his sword to cleave it in two. To his surprise, the ball fell into two halves and a lively, small boy came out from between, glistening with gold. This both amazed and delighted Li Jing.

这时，一位名叫太乙真人的道长登门求见。李靖忙把他请了进来。太乙真人一见李靖，便问道："听说贵府新添了一位公子，特来贺喜。可否抱来一见？"李靖说："这孩子一出生就与众不同，我正为此事疑惑呢。"他便叫人把孩子抱了出来。

太乙真人见了小孩，给他取名哪吒，收他为徒，并送给他两件礼物。李靖接过一看，一件是金光闪闪的镯子，叫做乾坤圈，一件是光彩夺目的红绫，叫做混天绫。

Just at this moment, a Taoist priest by the name of Taiyi the Immortal arrived to visit the family and was warmly welcomed by Li Jing. Greeting Li Jing, the visitor said, "I've just learned that you've got a new baby. Congratulations! Can I have a look at him?"

"He came out in an extraordinary manner. I've just been wondering about it," Li Jing replied and asked somebody to bring the baby.

Seeing the infant, Taiyi named him Nezha and decided to apprentice him. He also gave the boy two gifts which Li Jing received on his son's behalf. One of the gifts was a gold bracelet known as the Ring of the Universe, and the other was a piece of silk in brilliant red known as the Ribbon of the Heavens.

一转眼,哪吒已经七岁了,本领过人,还学会了三头六臂的功夫。

一天,他外出游玩。一路上看见土地干涸,庄稼都枯死了。他拉住一位愁眉苦脸的老农一问,才知道东海龙王不管老百姓的死活,几个月滴雨未下,还经常派出夜叉到海边强抢童男童女。哪吒听后十分气愤。

这时忽然人群四散奔逃,有人喊:"快跑,夜叉来了!"

Time flew. Nezha was now seven years old, and had developed superhuman powers through exercise.

One day when he went on an outing, he saw parched farmland and crops withering due to drought. Taking the hand of a woebegone old farmer, he asked the cause. "The Dragon King of the Eastern Sea (Donghai) is simply not concerned with our lives," the old farmer explained. "He has not only withheld the rain for several months, but from time to time he also sends Yaksha ashore to seize boys and girls in the night." Nezha became outraged at this.

Just then he saw people running in all directions. "Gee up! Here comes the Yaksha," one of them cried.

哪吒定睛一看，只见一个蓝头发红面乳的夜叉浮出海面，龇牙咧嘴地朝岸边游来。哪吒冲到海边，大叫一声："大胆夜叉，不得伤人！"夜叉见一个小娃娃竟敢对自己大喊大叫，举起手中的大斧砍了过来。哪吒不慌不忙地躲过一招，拿出手上的乾坤圈向夜叉抛去。夜叉被乾坤圈砸中脑袋，当场毙命。

　　Casting his eyes toward the sea, Nezha saw the blue-haired and red-faced Yaksha rising up from the waves and swimming toward the shore, its ferocious fangs sticking out from a fierce-looking mouth. Rushing toward the seaside, Nezha shouted, "No harm to the villagers, you devil!" Seeing it was a small boy cursing him, the Yaksha raised his axe to overpower Nezha. Effortlessly, Nezha dodged the cut. He then took out his Ring of the Universe and flung it at the Yaksha. Struck on the head, the Yaksha instantly dropped dead.

得知夜叉被杀的消息,龙王三太子率领一群虾兵蟹将前来报仇。见哪吒只是一个小孩子,三太子根本没把他放在眼里,举枪就刺。哪吒往旁一闪身,抖动混天绫,混天绫化作一团团火焰,将三太子围在中间,动弹不得。哪吒又掏出乾坤圈,奋力一扔,正中三太子面门。

三太子应声倒地,现出原形,原来是一条小龙。哪吒用脚踩住小龙,剥了龙皮,抽出龙筋,一路摆弄着回家去了。

At the news of the Yaksha's death, the Dragon King's third son led his underlings to take revenge on Nezha. Seeing that Nezha was but a small child, he grew haughty and thrust his spear toward the boy. Nezha stepped to one side and shook his Ribbon of the Heavens. Instantly, it turned into numerous fireballs to box up the Dragon King's third son. Nezha then took out his Ring of the Universe and flung it at him.

The Dragon King's third son was hit square in the face. He fell to the ground and betrayed his true self--a dragonet. Trapping the dragonet beneath one of his feet, Nezha peeled off its skin and pulled out its tendons. He then set off for home, playing with his trophies on the way.

东海龙王听说三太子死了，暴跳如雷，发誓要找哪吒算账。他来到李靖家中，说了事情的经过。李靖不相信，便去找哪吒问话。到后院一看，哪吒正在玩龙筋，这才明白儿子真的闯祸了。李靖带着哪吒来给东海龙王陪罪，龙王不依不饶，声称要到天庭玉皇大帝那里去告状。

At the news of his third son's death, the Dragon King stamped with fury. He vowed to avenge his son on Nezha. He came to Li Jing's home and told his host the whole story. Li Jing would not believe it and went to question Nezha. In the backyard, he saw Nezha playing with the tendons. Now convinced of his son's wrongdoing, Li Jing brought Nezha before the Dragon King to atone for the misbehavior. But the Dragon King would not forgive him and threatened to bring the case to the Jade Emperor, the supreme celestial ruler.

哪吒找师父借了隐身符，早早来到南天门等候。他看到东海龙王到了南天门，可东海龙王却看不到他。哪吒拿起乾坤圈将东海龙王打倒在地，这才现出身形，大喊道："看你还敢不敢告状！"

龙王又羞又恼，大叫："就是要告，绝不饶你！"哪吒见他不肯让步，就动手去撕他身上的鳞片，一会儿就撕下了四五十片，痛得东海龙王连连告饶："求求你，快住手！我不告了，不告了！"哪吒怕东海龙王逃走，就把他变成一条小蛇，放在袖子里带回家中。李靖夫妇一见儿子又闯了祸，忙叫他赶快放了龙王。东海龙王气极败坏地说："我要找四海龙王一起来报仇。等着瞧！"说完，一溜烟地走了。

Nezha went to his master who gave him a stealth cloak. Then he went early to wait by the southern gate of the Heavenly Palace. He saw the Dragon King coming to the gate, but the King could not see him in his stealth cloak. Nezha flung his Ring of the Universe against the Dragon King and knocked him down. Now revealing himself before his adversary, Nezha said, "Do you still dare to tell the Jade Emperor on me?"

Shamed and angry, the Dragon King replied, "Absolutely! I'll never let you go unpunished." Seeing that the Dragon King would not back down, Nezha reached out to peel off his scales and tore off scores of them in a minute. Badly hurt, the Dragon King begged Nezha for mercy. "Stop, please. I'll not tell on you any more." For fear that the Dragon King might run away, Nezha turned him into a snake and brought it home. For fear of new trouble, Nezha's parents asked him to free the Dragon King. Once free, the Dragon King sputtered to Nezha, "I'll bring the dragon kings from the other seas to help in my revenge. Wait for it!" This said, he fled like lightning.

第二天，东海龙王果然召集了西海龙王、南海龙王、北海龙王，带着一群虾兵蟹将前来兴师问罪。他们发起滔滔洪水，淹了陈塘关，扬言如不交出哪吒绝不罢休。

哪吒想出去和龙王们决一死战。李靖怕惹出事端，训斥道："还嫌你闯的祸不够多吗？"他命令手下收去了混天绫和乾坤圈两件宝物，不准哪吒出去应战。

As he had vowed, the following day the Dragon King of the East China Sea brought the kings of the west, south and north seas and an army of underlings to make a punitive expedition against Nezha. They raised a flood to submerge the Chentangguan Pass and threatened never to stop the flooding until the villagers handed Nezha over to them.

Nezha asked to be allowed to go and fight against the invaders but was forbidden to do so by his father. "No more trouble!" his father ordered, and disarmed Nezha of his Ring of the Universe and Ribbon of the Heavens to prevent him from fighting.

洪水滔天,眼见着城池被淹,百姓就要流离失所。李靖带哪吒来到城门前,要拔剑砍下儿子的头颅向龙王谢罪。周边的百姓纷纷跪下,替他求情。

哪吒不愿看见全城百姓受苦,他平静地说道:"父亲母亲,孩儿不孝,闯下大祸,连累了父母和众乡亲。我一人做事一人当,愿以死相还。我死后割肉还母,剔骨还父,以报答你们的养育之恩。"说完便拔出宝剑自刎身亡。

Towering waves were rolling in. The whole town was in peril of sinking under the floods at any moment, and its residents would become destitute and homeless as a result. Li Jing brought Nezha to the town gate. As an earnest proof of his apology to the Dragon King, he offered to behead his son who had stirred up all the trouble. Just as Li Jing raised his sword, the residents in the town dropped to their knees to plead for Nezha.

Hating to see the people suffering for him, Nezha went to his parents and 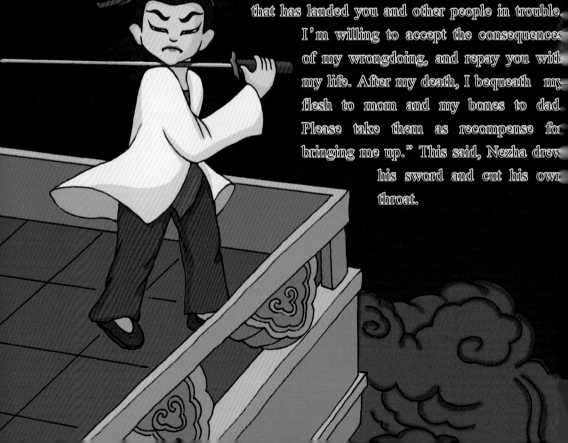 said calmly, "My dear father and mother, I know I'm not an obedient child. It is my misbehavior that has landed you and other people in trouble. I'm willing to accept the consequences of my wrongdoing, and repay you with my life. After my death, I bequeath my flesh to mom and my bones to dad. Please take them as recompense for bringing me up." This said, Nezha drew his sword and cut his own throat.

哪吒的师父太乙真人听说哪吒的死讯并不悲伤,他不慌不忙地到池塘里采起莲藕和莲花来。他把莲藕和莲花摆成一个人的形状,叫道:"哪吒,醒来,快醒来。"只见那小人顿时活了过来,竟是活蹦乱跳的哪吒。太乙真人又送了哪吒两件宝物,一件是风火轮,踏上它日行万里;一件是火尖枪,锋利无边威力无穷。得了宝物,哪吒的本领更大了。

When told the news of Nezha's death, Taiyi the Immortal, Nezha's master, did not show any grief. Calmly he went to a pond nearby and picked some lotus roots and flowers. He put them together in the shape of a human being and called to it, "Now wake up, Nezha. Be quick." Immediately, the figure he produced came to life. It was none other than the lively Nezha. Taiyi then gave Nezha two new gifts: the Wheel of Wind and Fire, which could travel thousands of miles a day, and the Flame-pointed Spear. With these two weapons, Nezha became even more powerful.

哪吒起死回生之后,到家中取了混天绫和乾坤圈,踩了风火轮,提了火尖枪,直奔东海而去。龙王见哪吒找上门来,大惊失色,忙招呼虾兵蟹将出来抵挡。

哪吒神勇无比,如入无人之境,只打得虾兵蟹将连滚带爬,四散奔逃。他拿起混天绫一抢,龙宫里地动山摇,晃动不止,各种物件翻落在地,乱成一片。

东海龙王吓得缩成一团,哪吒冲上前去,揪住龙角,道:"看你还仗势欺人不?天下大旱,快些降雨,这样就能饶你不死!"龙王连连告饶,急忙化作真龙腾云布雨。大雨从天而降,百姓一片欢呼。哪吒高兴地笑了。

Nezha went home to pick up his Ring of the Universe and Ribbon of the Heavens. Bringing the three magic weapons with him, he rushed to the Eastern Sea on the Wheel of Wind and Fire. Panic-stricken at the sight of Nezha, the Dragon King immediately mustered his underlings for support.

But they proved no match for the valiant Nezha. Wherever Nezha reached, his enemies either fell in rows or fled in panic. Nezha then spread his Ribbon of the Heavens. Immediately, the Dragon King's palace began to quake violently and everything in it fell to the ground.

The Dragon King huddled in abject fear. Nezha ran to him. Clutching his horn, Nezha asked, "Dare you continue your bullying everyone in the future? People have been suffering from a lasting drought. Send them some rain, or I'll kill you."

"I'll send them rain. Don't kill me, please," the Dragon King begged. He then turned himself into a real dragon and flew into the sky to spread rain. A downpour came. The locals burst into cheers, and Nezha smiled in joy.

完

End